Snowy the Rabbit

by Stephen Hynard, illustrated by Frances Thatcher

For Cathy (Stephen) For Jean and Roy (Fran)

CHILDRENS PRESS INTERNATIONAL

1983 edition published by Childrens Press International. A Terrapin book originally published by Hambleside Publishers Limited, Winchester, England. Text © 1980 by Stephen Hynard. Illustrations © 1980 by Frances Thatcher.

Library of Congress Cataloging in Publication Data

Hynard, Stephen.
   Snowy the rabbit.

(Stories to learn by)
Includes index.
Summary: Disturbed because so many of his relatives have the same name as he, Snowy tries to make himself a different color.
   [1. Color—Fiction.   2.   Rabbits—Fiction]   I.   Thatcher, Frances, ill.   II.   Title.   III.   Series.
PZ7.H988Sn   1983   [E]   82-22108
ISBN 0-516-08942-0   AACR2

"Mommy, why am I called Snowy?" asked Snowy the rabbit one morning. "Because you are white like the snow," said Mother Rabbit.

"But Snowy is such a boring name. There is cousin Snowy who lives on the hill, Grandma Snowy who lives by the river, and Uncle Snowy who lives behind the hedge, and lots and lots more. Oh, I wish I had a different name," said Snowy.

"If I were a different color perhaps I would have a different name," he thought as he hopped off for his morning adventures.

The sun sparkled and the sky was blue all over. If only he was blue like the sky! But he couldn't touch the sky even though he tried jumping very high.

The grass was a lovely green but rolling in the grass didn't make him green. It didn't seem fair at all!

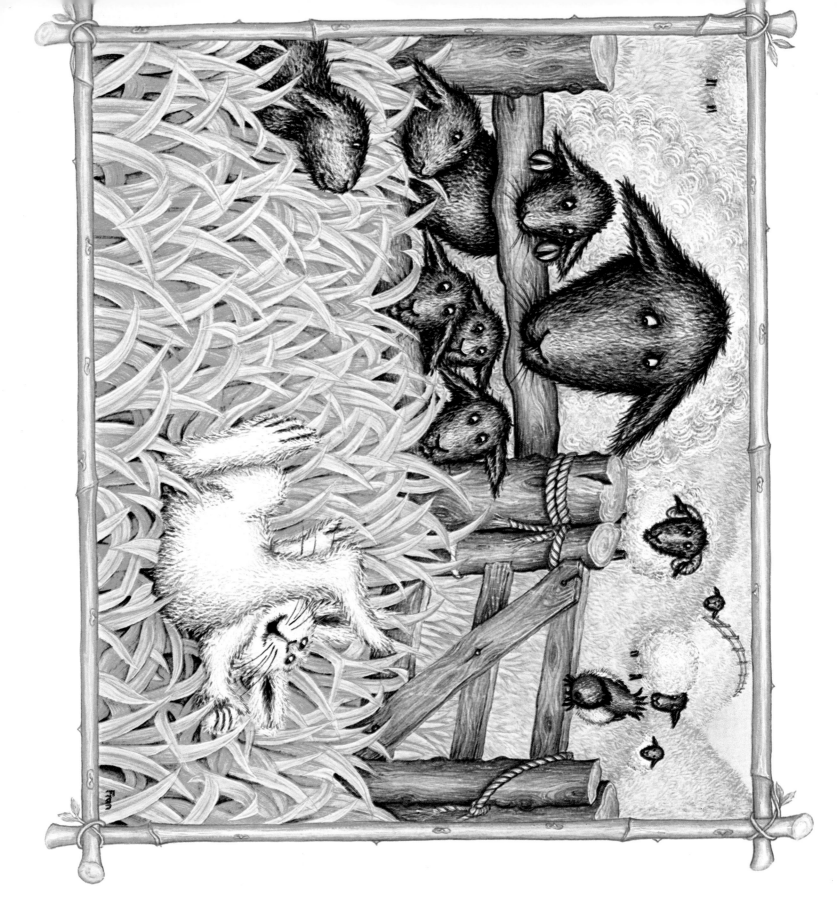

Then he had an idea. Mud!
Soon he was down by the river where
there was lots of lovely brown mud.
Snowy did not stop but jumped
straight in and rolled over and over.

It was so nice he wondered why his
grandma always told him not
to go near it.
"There," said Snowy, "now I'm a brown
rabbit. My name can be Browny."

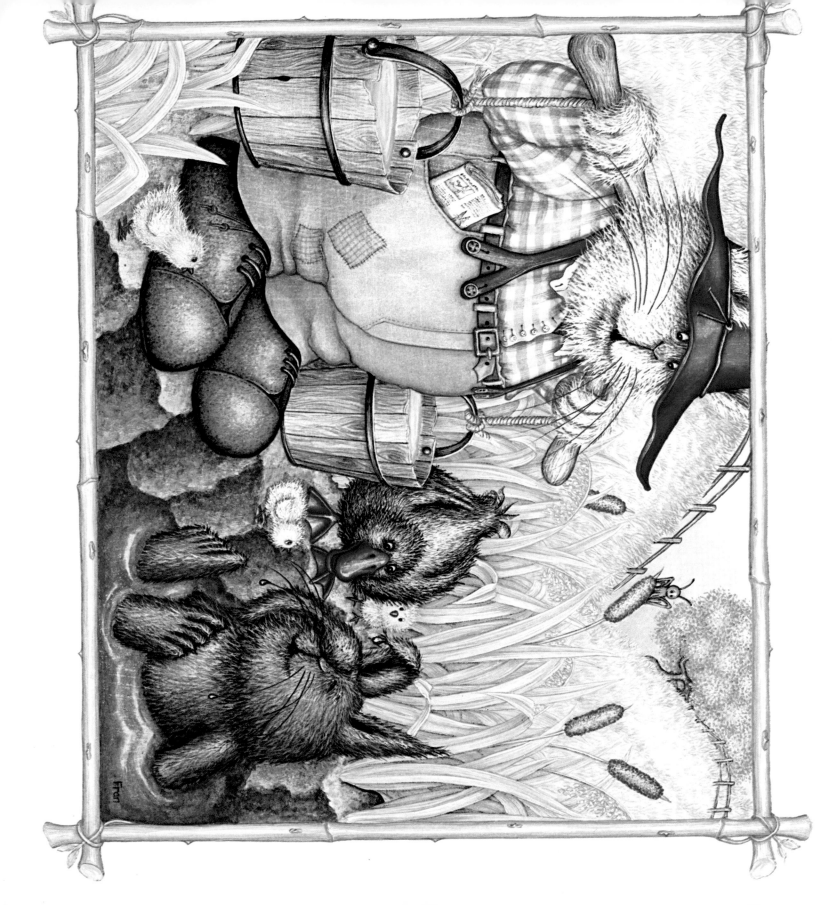

Snowy hopped off to see his grandma. "Who on earth is this?" wondered grandma. "Why, it is you, Snowy. You have been playing in the mud, you naughty rabbit."

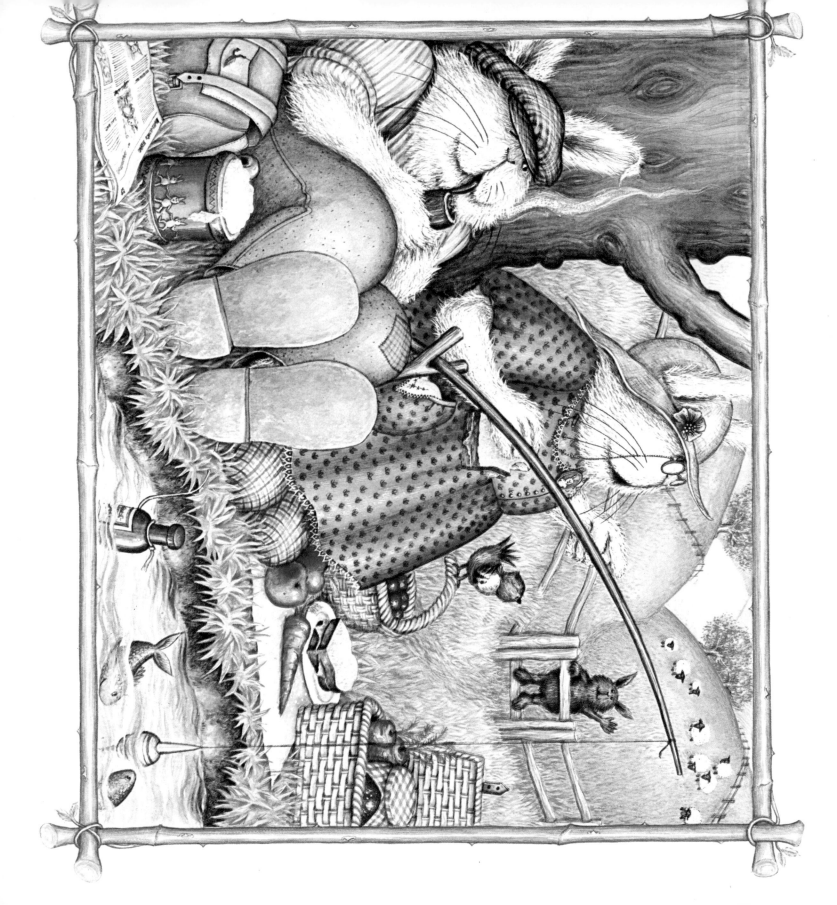

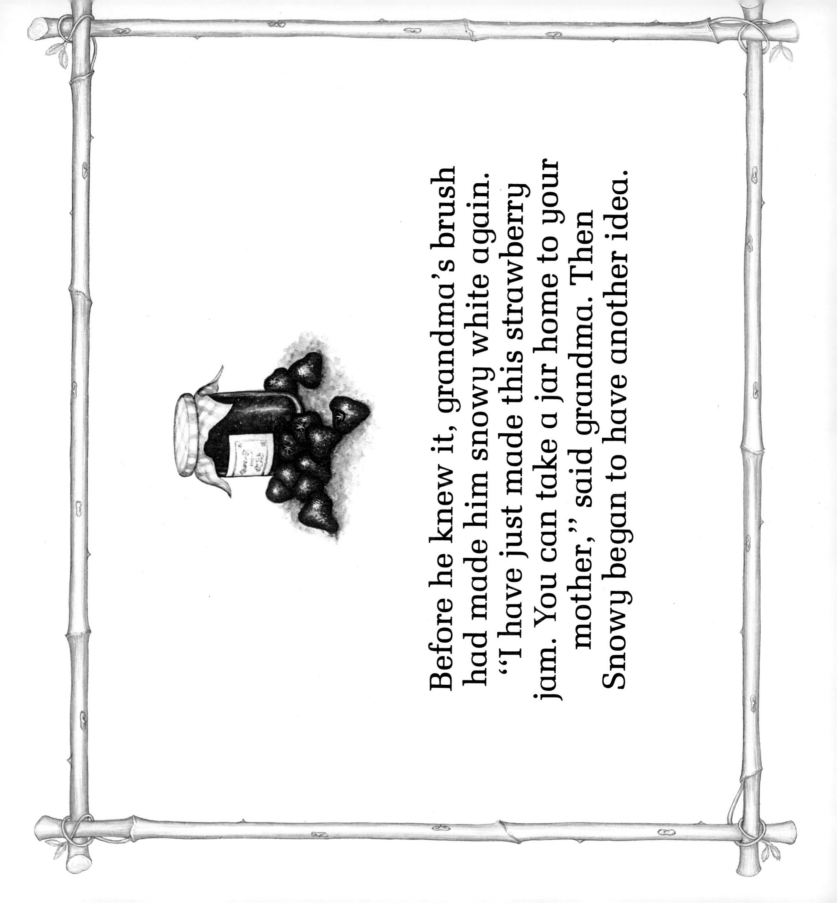

Before he knew it, grandma's brush had made him snowy white again. "I have just made this strawberry jam. You can take a jar home to your mother," said grandma. Then Snowy began to have another idea.

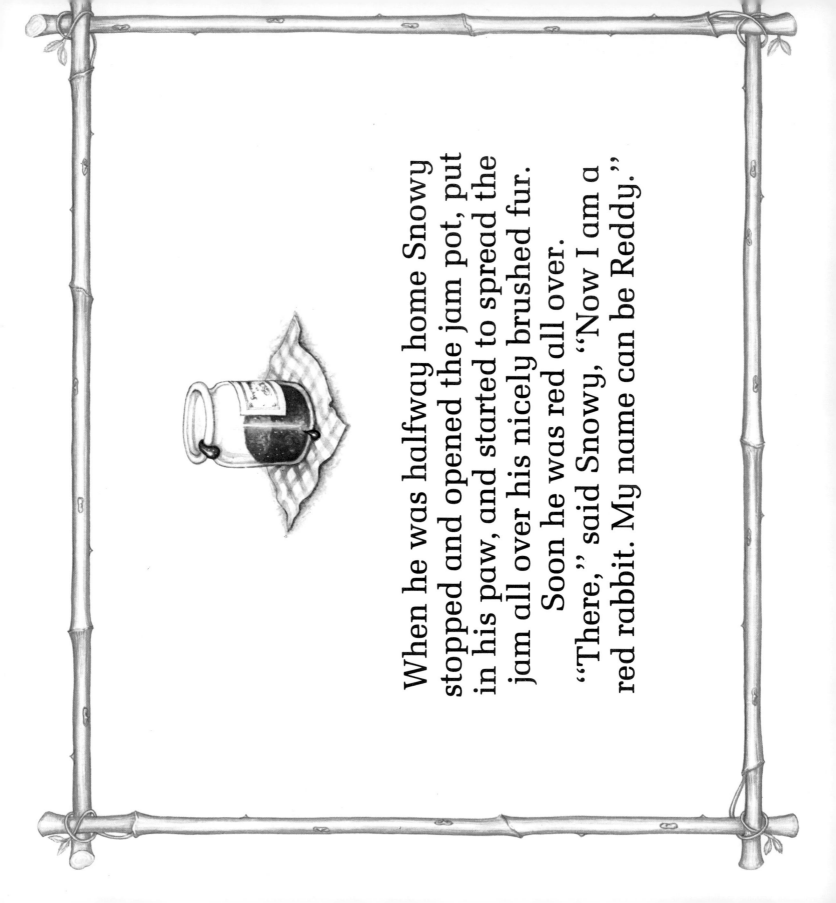

When he was halfway home Snowy stopped and opened the jam pot, put in his paw, and started to spread the jam all over his nicely brushed fur.

Soon he was red all over.

"There," said Snowy, "Now I am a red rabbit. My name can be Reddy."

No sooner had he said this when four of his friends came along. "What is that red thing?" they cried. "Why, it's a rabbit covered in jam . . . it's Snowy!" Then they licked the delicious jam off Snowy. And when Snowy was clean they finished the WHOLE POT!

Snowy was sad. He was still white, and he was also upset because he had lost all the jam. He went home to tell his mother. She was so cross that she made him stay and help her in the kitchen for the rest of the morning, so that he could not get into any more mischief.

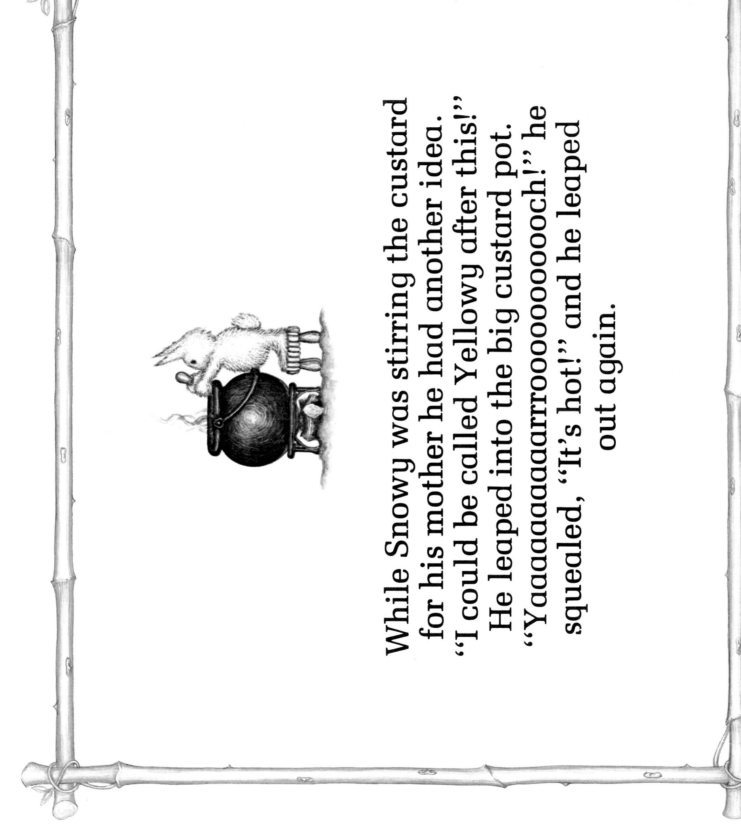

While Snowy was stirring the custard for his mother he had another idea. "I could be called Yellowy after this!" He leaped into the big custard pot. "Yaaaaaaaarrroooooooooch!" he squealed, "It's hot!" and he leaped out again.

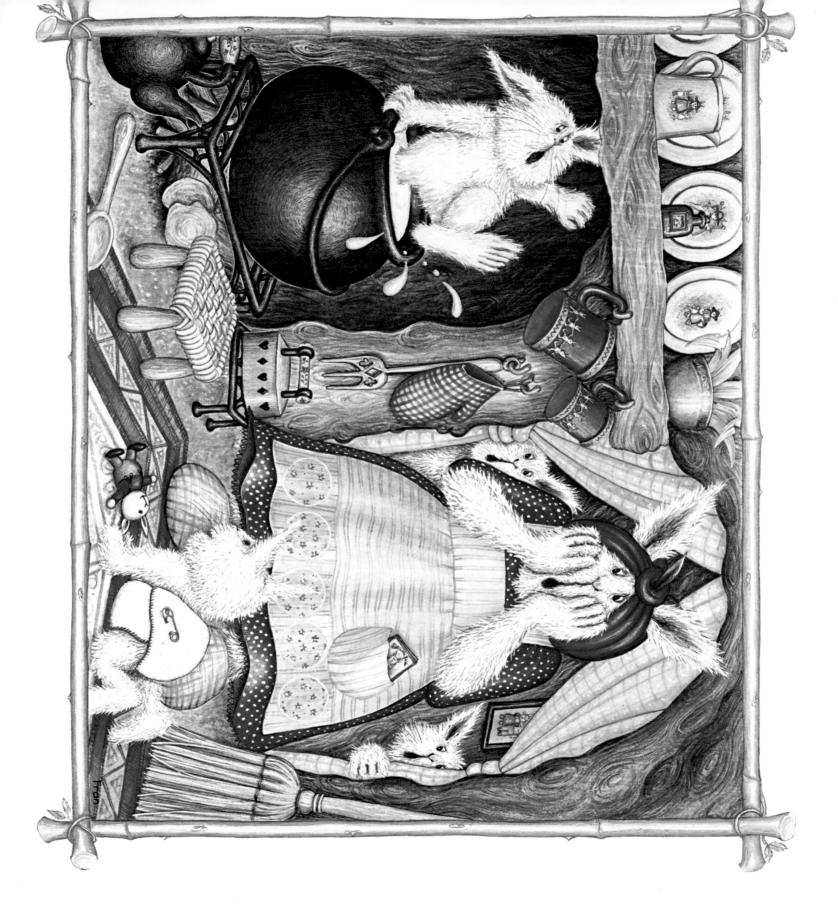

Mother Rabbit grabbed Snowy by his ears and threw him into a cold deep puddle. She scrubbed the custard from Snowy's fur and a very wet but white Snowy came out.

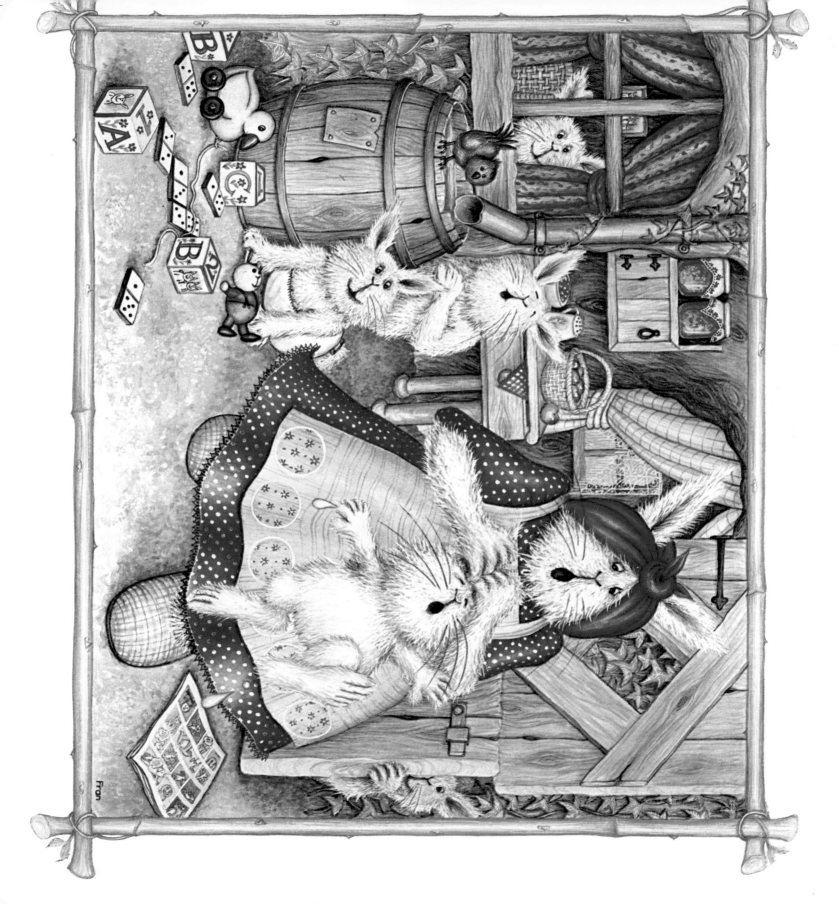

Snowy sat quietly in front of the fire. He was sad because none of his ideas had worked. Then Mother Rabbit came along with the dinner. "I've been thinking about what you said this morning, and I thought that as you are still a young rabbit I could give you another name."

"What?" asked Snowy.

"NAUGHTY Snowy!" Then they both laughed and laughed.

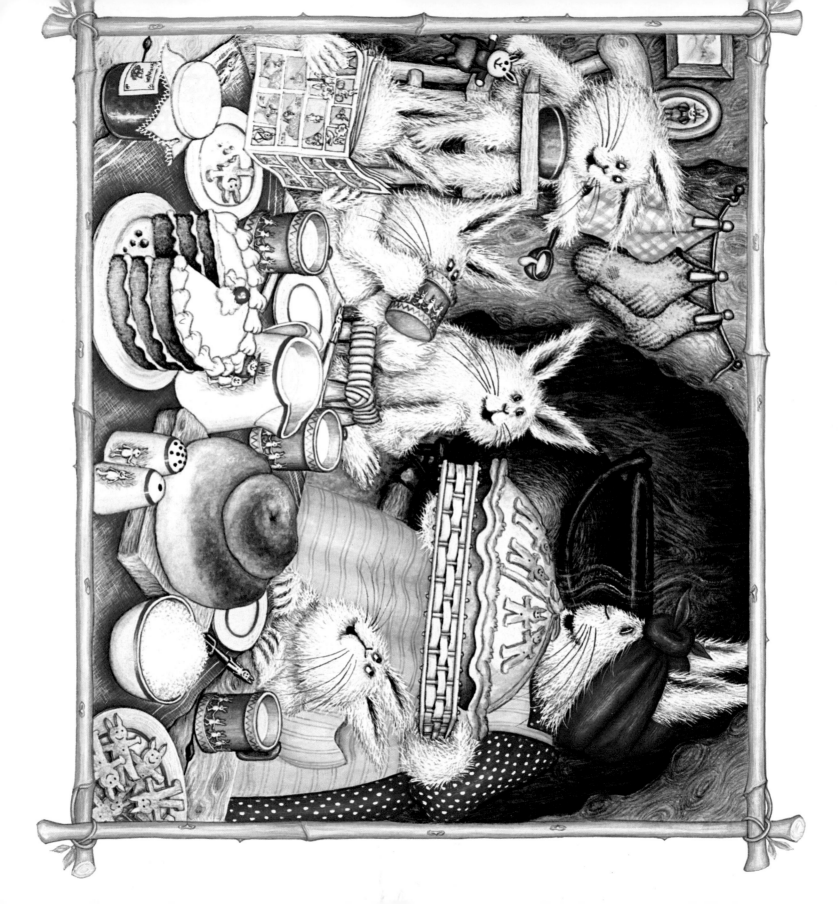

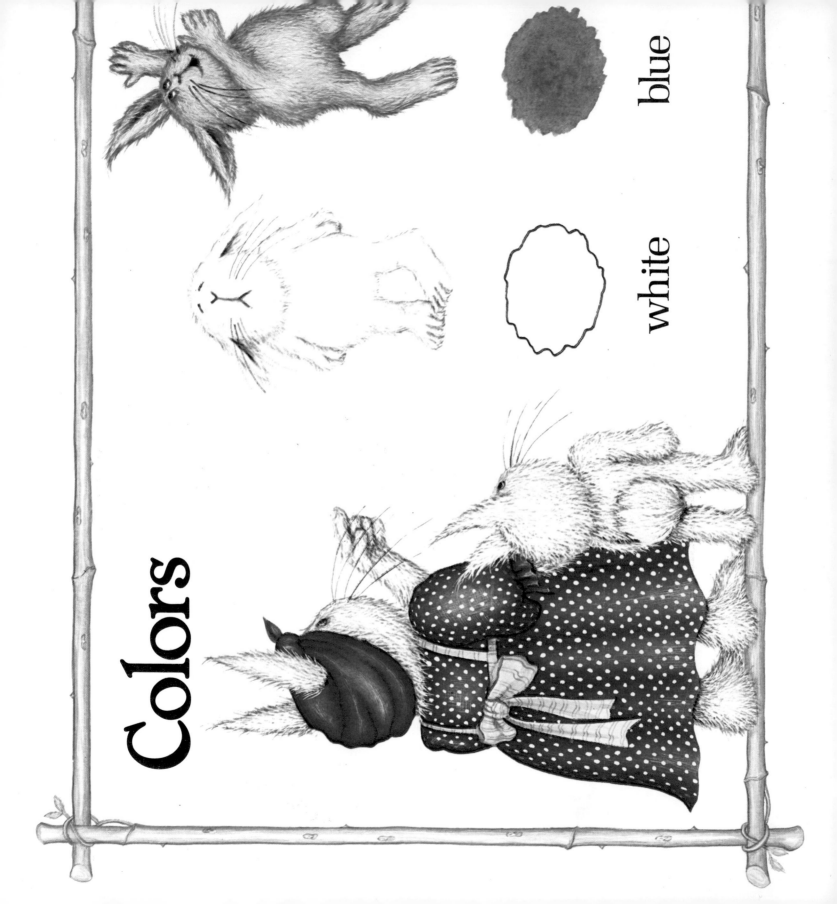

Colors

blue

white

green

brown

red

yellow

DUE DATE

OCT. 1 3 1992			
DEC. 6 1992			
JUL. 29 1993			
FEB. 1994			
MAR. 2 1994			
FEB. 1 3 1995			
MAR. 1 5 1995			
APR 0 9 1995			
MAY 1 7 1995			
OCT 1 1 '95			
DEC 1 5 '96			
MAR 2 5 '97			
APR 1 4 2000			
DEC 0 9 2010			
JAN 3 1 2010			
FEB 2 2 2011			

Printed in USA